www.enchantedlion.com

First American Edition, published in 2017 by Enchanted Lion Books
67 West Street, 317A, Brooklyn, NY 11222
Written originally in Korean and English by Nari Hong
Text and illustrations copyright © 2017 by Nari Hong
Design and layout: Marc Drumwright
Originally published in South Korea as 아빠, 미안해하지 마세요!
All rights reserved under International and Pan-American Copyright Conventions
A CIP record is on file with the Library of Congress
ISBN 978-159270-233-6
Printed in China by R.R. Donnelley Asia Printing Solutions

First Printing

Days With Dad

Nari Hong

ENCHANTED LION BOOKS
NEW YORK

This is my dad.

Dad can't walk.

He hasn't been able to since he was a baby.

He often says "I'm sorry" to me.

One day, Dad says, "I'm sorry I can't go bike riding with you."

"Oh, it's okay," I say.

"I love going to the park and looking at flowers with you."

One day, Dad says,
"Sweetie, I'm sorry
I can't go skating with you."

"Don't worry, Dad," I tell him.

"Ice fishing together
is much more fun!"

Another time at the beach, Dad says,
"Little One, I'm sorry I can't go
into the ocean with you."

"Don't worry, Dad," I say.

"It's great making sandcastles with you."

One day, Dad tells me,
"I'm sorry I can't play soccer with you."

"So what?" I say.

"What I really love is singing along with your ukulele."

When it rains, Dad says,
"Don't you want to splash
around in the puddles?"

And I say,
"No, not really, Dad."

"I love your rainy day cocoa much more."

Sometimes my friends talk about going on ski trips with their dads.

Or taking a banana boat.

So I tell them what an amazing chef my dad is.
And how fun it is to draw with him.

He also knows the names of all kinds of birds.
And animals always want to be friends with him.

Sometimes my dad worries about me...

...but I'm just happy being with him every single day.